Series 606D
A Ladybird Easy-Reading Book

© Ladybird Books Ltd (formerly Wills & Hepworth Ltd) 1968
All rights reserved. No part of this publication may be reproduced, stored in a retrieval system, or transmitted in any form or by any means, electronic, mechanical, photo-copying, recording or otherwise, without the prior consent of the copyright owner.

'WELL-LOVED TALES'

The Three Billy-goats Gruff

A LADYBIRD 'EASY-READING' BOOK

retold by VERA SOUTHGATE, M.A., B.Com.
with illustrations by ROBERT LUMLEY

Ladybird Books Ltd Loughborough

THE THREE BILLY-GOATS GRUFF

Once upon a time there were three billy-goats called Gruff.

7214 0222 4

One fine day, the three billy-goats Gruff set off up the hillside. They were going to look for some sweet grass to eat so that they could grow fat.

On the way up the hillside, the three billy-goats Gruff came to a river. On the other side of the river was a beautiful meadow. In the meadow was the finest grass they had ever seen.

There was a wooden bridge over the river. Under the bridge there lived an ugly troll. People were afraid to cross the bridge because of the troll. Every time he heard footsteps on the bridge, he popped out and gobbled up the person who was trying to cross.

The three billy-goats Gruff were very frightened at the thought of the troll. Yet they longed to eat the sweet grass in the meadow, on the other side of the river.

After a while, the youngest billy-goat Gruff said that he would be the first to try to cross the bridge.

Trip, trap, trip, trap, went the hooves of the youngest billy-goat Gruff on the wooden bridge.

Out popped the troll's ugly head. He was so ugly that the youngest billy-goat Gruff nearly fell down with fright.

"Who's that trip-trapping over my bridge?" roared the troll.

The youngest billy-goat Gruff spoke in a tiny voice. "It's only me, the littlest billy-goat Gruff," he said. "I'm going to the meadow to make myself fat."

"Then I'm coming to gobble you up," roared the troll.

"Oh! No! Please don't gobble me up," said the youngest billy-goat Gruff, in a tiny voice. "I'm far too little and not at all fat. Wait until the second billy-goat Gruff comes along. He's much fatter than I am."

"Very well," said the troll. "Be off with you! I'll wait until the second billy-goat Gruff comes along."

So the youngest billy-goat Gruff crossed the bridge and skipped off into the meadow to eat the sweet grass.

Then the second billy-goat Gruff said that he would try to cross the bridge.

Trip, trap, trip, trap, went the hooves of the second billy-goat Gruff on the wooden bridge.

Out popped the troll's ugly head. He was so ugly that the second billy-goat Gruff nearly fell down with fright.

"Who's that trip-trapping over my bridge?" roared the troll.

The second billy-goat Gruff spoke in a rather soft voice. "It's only me, the second billy-goat Gruff," he said. "I'm going to the meadow to make myself fat."

"Then I'm coming to gobble you up," roared the troll.

"Oh! No! Please don't gobble me up," said the second billy-goat Gruff, in his rather soft voice. "I'm not very big and I'm not very fat. Wait until the third billy-goat Gruff comes along. He's very big and very fat."

"Very well," said the troll. "Be off with you! I'll wait until the third billy-goat Gruff comes along."

So the second billy-goat Gruff crossed the bridge and skipped off into the meadow to eat the sweet grass.

Then, at last, up came the eldest billy-goat Gruff, to try to cross the bridge.

He was a very big billy-goat. His beard was long and his horns were almost fully grown.

TRIP, TRAP, TRIP, TRAP, BANG, BANG, BANG, BANG, went the hooves of the eldest billy-goat Gruff on the wooden bridge.

Out popped the troll's ugly head. He was so ugly that the eldest billy-goat Gruff nearly fell down with fright. But he did not show it. He only stamped his hooves harder—TRIP, TRAP, TRIP, TRAP, BANG, BANG, BANG, BANG!

“Who’s that trip-trapping over my bridge?” roared the troll.

The eldest billy-goat Gruff’s voice was even louder and gruffer than the troll’s voice. “It’s me, the biggest billy-goat Gruff,” he bellowed.

"Then I'm coming to gobble you up," roared the troll.

"Oh no you are not!" bellowed the eldest billy-goat Gruff. "I am coming to gobble *you* up!"

And he stamped his feet even louder; TRIP, TRAP, TRIP, TRAP, BANG, BANG, BANG, BANG!

After that, the eldest billy-goat Gruff butted the troll with his big horns. The troll fell off the bridge and into the river.

The ugly troll fell head first into the deep water. There was a mighty splash and he did not come up again.

So that was the end of the ugly troll.

From that time on, people went over the bridge without fear. Never again did the troll pop his head out from under the bridge to roar, “Who’s that trip-trapping over my bridge?”

Then the three billy-goats Gruff lived happily in the meadow on the hillside. They ate the sweet grass and they really did get fat.

Series 606D
A Ladybird Easy-Reading Book